Number Four, Bobby Orr!

by Mike Leonetti

illustrations by Shayne Letain

RAINCOAST BOOKS

Vancouver

First published in 2003 by Raincoast Books

Raincoast Books acknowledges the ongoing financial support of the Government of Canada through The Canada
Council for the Arts and the Book Publishing Industry Development Program (BPIDP); and the Government of British
Columbia through the BC Arts Council.

Edited by Scott Steedman

NATIONAL LIBRARY OF CANADA CATALOGUING IN PUBLICATION DATA
Leonetti, Mike, 1958–
    Number four, Bobby Orr! / Mike Leonetti ; Shayne Letain, illustrator.

    ISBN 1-55192-551-6 (bound). — ISBN 1-55192-671-7 (pbk).

    1. Orr, Bobby, 1948– —Juvenile fiction. I. Letain, Shayne. II. Title.
PS8573.E58734N85 2003   jC813'.54   C2003-910296-3
PZ7.L55Nu 2003

LIBRARY OF CONGRESS CATALOGUE NUMBER: 2003091052

Raincoast Books   In the United States:
9050 Shaughnessy Street   Publishers Group West
Vancouver, British Columbia   1700 Fourth Street
Canada   V6P 6E5   Berkeley, California
www.raincoast.com   94710

Acknowledgements
The writer would like to thank Nate Greenberg, Maria Leonetti, Paul Patzkou and Kevin Vautour for their assistance. Books
by the following writers or former Bruins players were consulted: Hal Bock, Clark Booth, John Devaney, Craig MacInnis,
Mark Mulvoy, Johnny Bucyk, Gerry Cheevers, Phil Esposito, Ted Green, Bobby Orr and Derek Sanderson. Newspapers
archives consulted: *Record American*, *Patriot Ledger*, *Boston Herald*, *Globe and Mail*, *Toronto Star*, *Toronto Telegram*.
Videos reviewed: Boston Garden: Banner Years, 1969–70 Boston Bruins season highlights; Bobby Orr highlights. Magazine
consulted: *Hockey Digest*.

Printed and bound in Hong Kong, China by Book Art Inc., Toronto

10 9 8 7 6 5 4 3

It was a windy Saturday morning in early March. My Dad and I were making our way from our house on Chestnut Street to the hockey arena on Elm Street. The wind froze our faces as we walked, but we were so used to the cold we didn't mind at all. We both loved hockey so much, we would go just about **anywhere** for a game.

Today Dad was coming to watch my team, the Bruins, play the Rangers. All the teams in the league I played in had names just like the teams in the National Hockey League. I played defense and I loved to **rush** up the ice with the puck just like my favourite player, Bobby Orr of the Boston Bruins!

I was a hockey fan because of my Dad. He **loved** the Bruins. One day about three years ago, when I was just five years old, Dad bought me a pack of hockey cards. When I opened the pack the first card I saw was of Bobby Orr. It was the first hockey card I ever owned.

The front of the card had a photo of Bobby with a big smile. On the back was information about him, including the fact that he was born in Parry Sound, Ontario. The card also said that Bobby was "a rushing defenseman who can set up goals as well as score them." From that moment on, Bobby Orr became my favourite player, and hockey was the game I wanted to play.

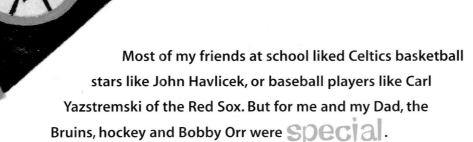

Most of my friends at school liked Celtics basketball stars like John Havlicek, or baseball players like Carl Yazstremski of the Red Sox. But for me and my Dad, the Bruins, hockey and Bobby Orr were special.

I began to collect everything I could about Bobby Orr and the Bruins. I looked out for cards of other Bruin players and soon had Eddie Johnston, Don Awrey and Ted Green. I got a poster of Bobby, and Mom bought me a Bruins pennant to hang next to it on my wall. Dad also gave me a bobbin head doll that he had bought a few years before.

Dad told me that the Bruins had not been a very successful team for years. But Bobby Orr had changed that, and now they were a contender for the **Stanley Cup!**

Back at the arena on Elm Street, my game against the Rangers was going well and we were winning 2–1. Even though I was not the biggest player, I could skate really well and I even scored one of our goals with a slapshot from the blueline.

We were still ahead late in the game when the puck went behind our net and I skated hard to pick it up. I could hear one of the Ranger players chasing me and just as I was reaching for the puck, I tripped over a stick. I tumbled into the boards behind the net.

I knew it was an accident, but there was a sharp pain in my leg. I could tell I was hurt because I could see my coach and Dad running out to me as I lay on the ice. Then I guess I must have passed out …

The next thing I remember was waking up in the hospital with my Mom sitting
beside me. My Dad was talking to a doctor.

"What happened, Mom?" I asked.

"The doctor had to operate on your leg because you injured it pretty badly"
she said, trying to smile.

I looked down and saw my leg in a cast.

"Can I go home now?" I asked.

My Dad and the doctor came over when they heard me.

"You're going to be fine, Joey, but the doctor wants to keep you here so they can
check your leg and see how it's mending," Dad said.

"How long will I have to stay? When does this cast come off?"

"One question at a time, Joey. I'm Doctor Williams and everything is going to be
all right. The operation went fine but we want to be sure, so we're going to keep
you here for a little while, OK?"

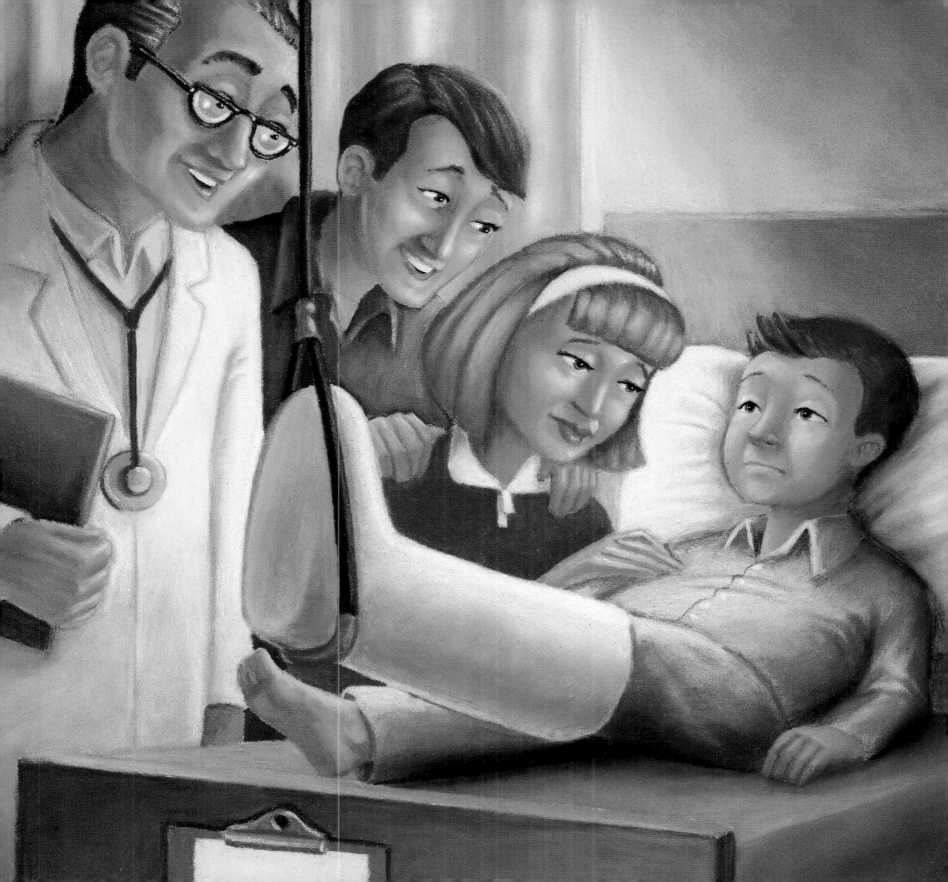

Everyone at the hospital was really nice to me, and Mom and Dad came to visit every day. But I would much rather have been at school and finishing the hockey season with my teammates. My Dad got me a TV for my room, so I was able to watch the Bruins games on channel 38 and listen to Don Earle doing the play-by-play.

The Bruins were having a great season and Bobby Orr was leading the NHL with the most points! No defenseman had ever done that before but Bobby was scoring some spectacular goals and making fantastic passes to his teammates. Everyone thought the Bruins had a great chance to win the Stanley Cup.

I had always wanted to write a letter to Bobby Orr and now that I had the time, I decided to do it. I would tell him how much I liked him and congratulate him on his great performance.

In my letter, I told Bobby that he was my favourite player and that I hoped the Bruins would do well in the playoffs. Then I asked him about being a defenseman. I hoped that he could give me some good tips because I was a defenseman, too.

I asked Dad if he could mail the letter for me, and if he thought Bobby would have the time to answer.

"Sure, Joey, I think Bobby will reply," Dad said. "But remember, he's pretty busy right now with the playoffs not far off."

A week went by and I still couldn't leave the hospital. I was getting pretty bored and sure wished I could play some real hockey. I knew Dad had tickets to the next Bruins game and I wanted to go really badly. It would be my first trip to the Boston Garden!

Dear Joey,

I really appreciate that you took the time to write to me. We can use all the fan support we can get if we're going to finish first and win the Stanley Cup! I hope you enjoy the photo that I've included with this letter.

Sincerely, Bobby Orr

A few days later I got a letter from Bobby Orr. It came with an autographed photo and he said he really appreciated that I took the time to write to him. He also said that the Bruins needed all the fan support they could get, because they wanted to finish first and Win the Stanley Cup.

"That's a nice letter and picture, Mom," I said. "But Bobby didn't give me any advice on how to play defense."

"Well Joey, Bobby is very busy right now so he probably doesn't have the chance to answer every question. I'm sure there are lots of boys and girls who write him letters every day."

"Yeah, I guess you're right. I'm going to save this letter and show it to all the kids at school when I get back," I replied. "Dad has tickets for the game tonight, right? Is he going?"

"He doesn't want to go without you Joey, because he promised to take you."

"No, Mom! Tell him to go, and you go with him. You both need a break from always coming to visit me here," I said, in an insisting sort of way.

That night Mom and Dad went to the game and I watched it on TV. The Bruins beat the Minnesota North Stars 5–0. Bobby scored two goals and added two assists and set a new record for most assists in one season when he got his 78th of the year. The crowd gave him a standing ovation. But the most exciting thing happened after the game when my parents came to see me.

"Joey, you'll never guess what happened," my Dad said excitedly. "After the game was over, we went to the car and found we had a flat tire. Well, I had to replace it and I was having a hard time getting the spare on when this young man came over to help. Take a guess who it was."

"Who?" I asked breathlessly.

"Bobby Orr! I didn't even realize it was him until your mother asked!"

"When I realized who it was, I told him about you Joey," Mom jumped in. "I told Bobby how you had just written him a letter. Well, guess what? He's coming to see you tomorrow afternoon, right after practice!"

I could hardly believe it! I was so excited I hardly slept a wink all night.

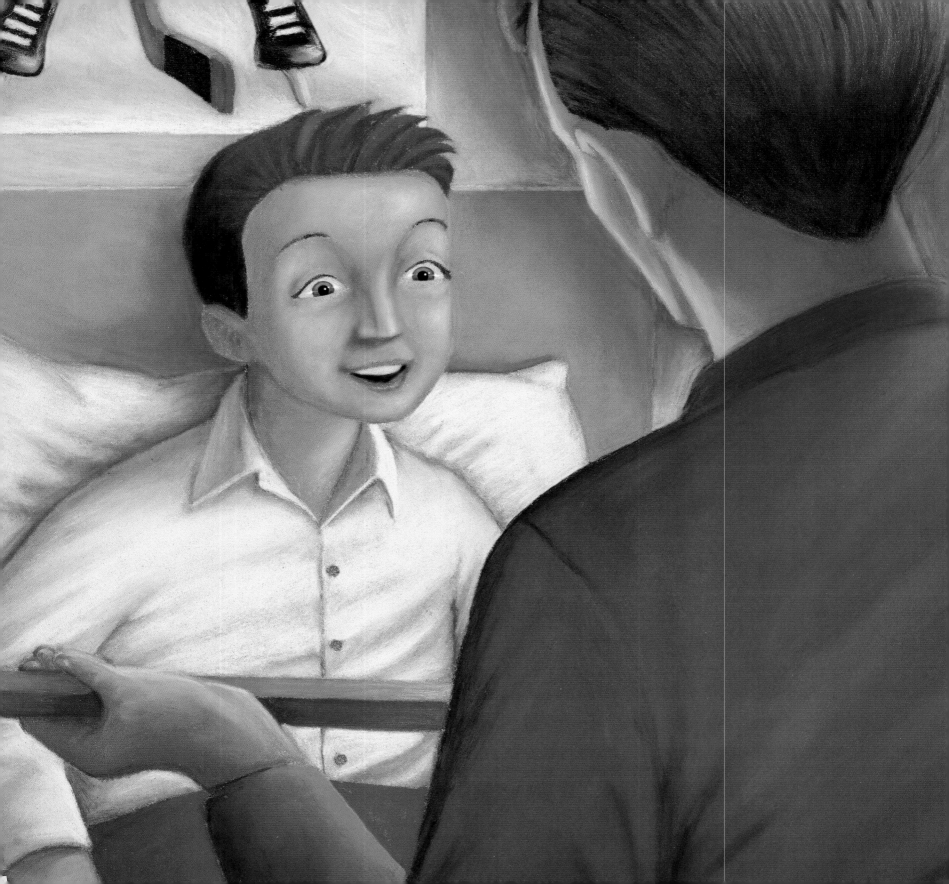

Just like he'd promised, Bobby Orr came to see me the next day. "Hi Joey," he said with a big smile as he came into my room. "I heard you had an accident playing hockey."

"Yes," I stammered, hardly able to speak and unable to beLieve my eyes!

"You know, I've had injuries to both my knees and I'm still playing hockey, so I hope you'll go back to play next season," Bobby said.

"Sure, I'm going to try Mr. Orr. But I'm a little on the small side and now I'll be worried about my leg," I answered.

"Joey, lots of people told me I was too small when I was your age. But I didn't let that stop me. I've had many operations on my legs much like the one you had, and I'm still playing."

Then Bobby took out the letter I had sent him. "Your Mom told me I forgot to give you some advice about how to play defense. Just remember, Joey, that skating is the skill you need to develop most. You should learn to turn in every direction." Before he left Bobby gave me a hockey stick signed by all the Bruins. I knew it was one of his because it had a single strip of black tape on the blade.

"Are the Bruins going to win the Cup, Mr. Orr?" I asked as he was heading out.

"We're confident we can do it, Joey, but it won't be easy. You keep cheering for us and get back to school as soon as you can."

"Yes, sir," I smiled.

I slept with Bobby Orr's stick beside me all night!

I finally got out of the hospital and eventually the cast came off my leg. Bobby finished the season with 120 points, more than any other player. The Chicago Black Hawks finished first in the eastern division, but when the playoffs started, the Bruins beat the New York Rangers and the Black Hawks! Then they met the St. Louis Blues in the Stanley Cup finals.

The Bruins won the first three games of the series easily and were ready to sweep their way to the Cup. The fourth game was going to be played on the Sunday afternoon of Mother's Day. I was making plans to watch it on TV with my Dad after we celebrated Mom's special day when a neighbour came running over to the house. It was Mr. Amico. He was a great Bruins fan and had a bumper sticker on his car that said "Bring the Cup Home!" He also had season tickets with up-close seats at the Garden.

"Hey Joey, how would you and your Dad like to go to the game this afternoon?" he asked.

"You're not going?" I answered, not believing what I'd heard.

"My Mom came a long way to be here for Mother's Day, so it wouldn't be very nice of me to leave her. I'll watch the game on TV with her. You go and bring home the Cup!"

I quickly found my Dad and told Mom what was happening. She waved us off with a smile. She knew how happy this would make us!

Dad and I took the train to the Garden. It was a fifteen-minute ride from our house and I enjoyed every second! Our seats were in lodge 15, numbers three and four in row A, right up against the glass near the Bruins bench. Naturally I took the ticket with number four on it, because that was Bobby's number.

There were over 14,000 fans crammed into the Garden and it was very hot, but everyone was in a good mood. I saw a huge banner that said "Go Bruins, Get That Cup!" Boston hadn't won the Cup in 29 years so the crowd was really excited. The atmosphere was electric!

GO BRUINS GET THE CUP

The game started and Bruins goalie Gerry Cheevers had to make a great save on Red Berenson of the Blues. Then the Bruins struck first when Derek Sanderson swept the puck out to defenseman Rick Smith, who blasted a shot into the Blues net! **Goal!** But before the end of the first period, the Blues had tied the game.

Early in the second period the Blues made it 2–1 and nearly scored another. This was not going to be easy. Luckily, Phil Esposito scored a goal right off a face-off to tie it for the Bruins. But the Blues struck back once again in the first minute of the third period. It looked like Boston was in real trouble.

With just over six minutes to play, Bruins winger Johnny McKenzie did some great digging and got the puck out to Johnny Bucyk. Bucyk put it in the net and the game was tied at 3–3. Nobody else could score before the end of the third period — not even Bobby Orr, who tried to take the puck end to end just before time ran out. But he didn't make it.

I said to my Dad, "This is **really exciting**. I hope Bobby gets the puck and makes one of his rushes and scores right in front us."

"That would be great," Dad said.

I could **barely sit still** waiting for the overtime period to start!

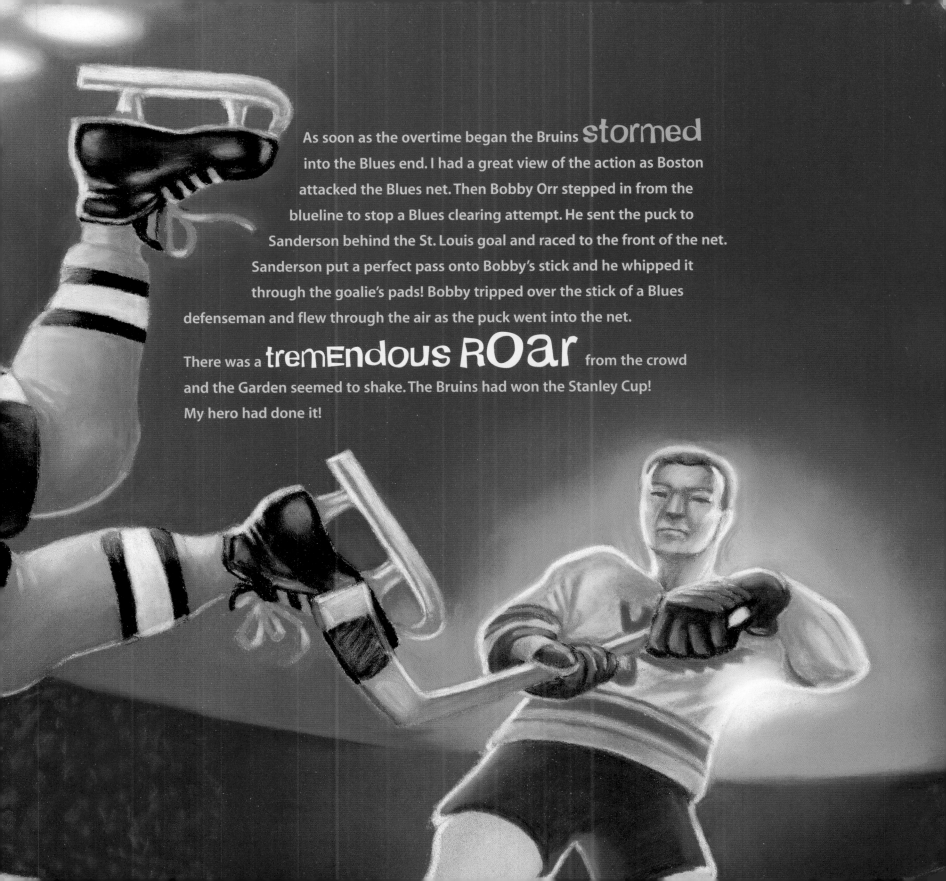

As soon as the overtime began the Bruins **stormed** into the Blues end. I had a great view of the action as Boston attacked the Blues net. Then Bobby Orr stepped in from the blueline to stop a Blues clearing attempt. He sent the puck to Sanderson behind the St. Louis goal and raced to the front of the net. Sanderson put a perfect pass onto Bobby's stick and he whipped it through the goalie's pads! Bobby tripped over the stick of a Blues defenseman and flew through the air as the puck went into the net.

There was a **tremEndous ROar** from the crowd and the Garden seemed to shake. The Bruins had won the Stanley Cup! My hero had done it!

My Dad and I jumped out of our seats and hugged as the Bruins mobbed Bobby Orr on the ice. They put Bobby and coach Harry Sinden on their shoulders. A shower of streamers and cups was raining down. Bruins Captain Johnny Bucyk accepted the shining Stanley Cup and skated around, holding it in the air.

We finally left the Garden and joined the party outside on Causeway Street. People were honking their car horns and calling out, "We're number one!" It was such a happy time for Bruins fans. My Dad and I enjoyed the celebration so much we decided to walk home. We smiled all the way!

By the beginning of the next hockey season, I was ready to play again. I was nervous before my first game even though my leg felt much better. My Dad encouraged me to get back on the ice and play again. I knew he was right. Early in the game the puck came to me and as it hit my stick I began to think about Bobby Orr and what he had said. He was right. If you are dedicated and willing, you can overcome just about anything. He had done it and maybe I could do it too. I took the puck up the ice as fast as I could, hoping I might score just like my hockey hero, number four, Bobby Orr!

About Bobby Orr

Bobby Orr joined the Boston Bruins as an 18-year-old in 1966. He promptly won the Calder Trophy as the best rookie in the NHL. In 1969–70, the season in which this story is set, Orr became the first player in history to win four major awards. He took the Hart Trophy as the NHL's most valuable player, the Norris Trophy as the best defenseman,

the Art Ross Trophy for recording the most points (120) and the Conn Smythe Trophy as the best player in the playoffs. He finished off his outstanding year by scoring the Stanley Cup-winning goal, a feat he repeated for the Bruins in 1972.

By the time his great career was over, Orr had won the Norris Trophy eight years in a row (1968 to 1975). He also won a second Art Ross (1974–75), another Conn Smythe (1972) and two more Hart trophies (1971 and 1972). In 657 games, Orr recorded 270 goals and 645 assists for 915 points. In 74 playoffs games he had 92 points (26 goals, 66 assists). Orr played courageously throughout his career despite knee injuries that caused him great pain. He was forced to retire in 1978. The following year he was elected to the Hall of Fame and the Bruins retired his famous "number four" sweater.

A shy man off the ice, Orr spent many hours visiting children in hospitals and working for charitable causes, as he still does today. One of the greatest players of all time, Orr is treasured by hockey fans everywhere but nowhere more than in his hometown of Parry Sound, and Boston, the site of his greatest triumphs.